Central

To read fluently is one of the basic aims of anyone learning English as a foreign language. **And it's never too early to start.** Ladybird Graded Readers are interesting but simple stories designed to encourage children between the ages of 6 and 10 to read with pleasure.

Reading is an excellent way of reinforcing language already acquired, as well as broadening a child's vocabulary. Ladybird Graded Readers use a limited number of grammatical structures and a carefully controlled vocabulary, but where the story demands it, a small number of words outside the basic vocabulary are introduced. In *Rapunzel* the following words are outside the basic vocabulary for this grade:

beautiful, begin, climb, grow up, hurt, ladder, lettuces, prince, silk, tears, tower

Further details of the structures and vocabulary used at each grade can be found in the Ladybird Graded Readers *leaflet.*

A list of books in the series can be found on the back cover.

British Library Cataloguing in Publication Data

Ullstein, Sue
    Rapunzel. — (English language teaching series).
    1. English language — Text-books for foreign speakers
    2. Readers — 1950-
    I. Title   II. Layfield, Kathie
    III. Grimm, Jacob. Rapunzel   IV. Series
    428.6'4   PE1128
    ISBN 0-7214-1049-9

First edition

Published by Ladybird Books Ltd Loughborough Leicestershire UK
Ladybird Books Inc Lewiston Maine 04240 USA

Printed in England

Rapunzel

written by Sue Ullstein
illustrated by Kathie Layfield

Ladybird Books

A man and his wife
are looking into a
witch's garden. They
can see some lettuces.

"Those lettuces are
good," the woman says.

"Yes, they are," the
man says. "I'll get
some for you."

"No, you mustn't,"
the woman says. "They're
the witch's lettuces."

But the woman likes
lettuces very much.
The next day she is
ill.

"Now I must get some
lettuces for you,"
the man says.

The man climbs into
the witch's garden.
He gets some lettuces.
He takes them home.
He gives them to his
wife.

She is very
happy.

The next day the man
climbs into the witch's
garden again. He
takes some lettuces.
But the witch sees
him. She is angry.

"Those are my lettuces,"
she says. "Give them
to me."

"Oh, please," the man
says. "My wife is
very ill. She needs
the lettuces."

"Yes," the witch says.
"You can have the
lettuces now. But
your wife is going to
have a baby. I want
that baby. You must
give it to me."

12

One day the woman has
a baby girl, Rapunzel.
The witch comes to
get the baby.

''Come with me,'' she says.

The man and his wife are
very sad. But they have
to give their baby
to the witch.

15

The witch takes Rapunzel
away. She puts her in a
tower. The tower has no door.
Rapunzel can never go out.
She grows up. She is a
beautiful woman, but she has
no friends. She is sad.

The witch sometimes
comes to see Rapunzel.
She goes to the tower
and she calls,
"Rapunzel, Rapunzel,
let down your hair."

19.

Rapunzel lets down her hair. The witch climbs up it.

One day a prince comes
to the tower. Rapunzel
is singing and he hears
her. He wants to go
into the tower, but
he cannot find a door.
Soon he goes away.

But the next day the prince goes back to the tower again. The witch comes. The prince sees the witch, but she does not see him.

She calls to Rapunzel, ''Rapunzel, Rapunzel, let down your hair!''

The prince watches
Rapunzel and the
witch. Rapunzel lets
down her hair. Then
the witch climbs up it.
She gets into the tower.

Soon the witch climbs
down Rapunzel's hair.
She goes away.

The prince goes to the
tower and calls,
"Rapunzel, Rapunzel,
let down your hair."

Rapunzel lets down
her hair again. The
prince climbs up it.
He gets into the tower.
Rapunzel is happy.
The prince is happy,
too. They talk and
talk and talk.

"Can I come and see
you again, Rapunzel?"
the prince asks.

"Yes, you can,"
Rapunzel says.

The prince often comes
to see Rapunzel.

One day he asks, ''Will
you marry me, Rapunzel?''

''Yes, I will,''
Rapunzel says. ''But
I can't marry you in
this tower. I must
get down, but there
is no door. Will
you help me?''

"Yes, I will," the prince says.

"Please bring me some silk," Rapunzel says. "I'll make a silk ladder. Then I can climb down the ladder."

The prince brings
Rapunzel some silk.
She begins to make a
ladder.

One day the witch comes to see Rapunzel again. She climbs up Rapunzel's hair, and she hurts her.

Rapunzel says, "You hurt me. The prince climbs up my hair, too. But he never hurts me."

The witch is very
angry. She cuts
Rapunzel's hair. She
takes her away.

Then the witch
sits in the tower.
She is waiting for the
prince.

The prince comes to
the tower.

"Rapunzel, Rapunzel,
let down your hair,"
he calls.

The witch has Rapunzel's
hair. She lets it
down.

The prince climbs up
the hair. He sees
the witch. She pushes
him down.

The tower is very
tall. The prince
hurts his head and
his eyes. He cannot
see.

The prince wants to find Rapunzel. He walks for days and days.

One day he
hears a girl. She is
singing. It is
Rapunzel.

"My prince!" Rapunzel says.
Happy tears come to
Rapunzel's eyes, and she
runs to him. Her tears
go into his eyes.

"Oh! I can see again," he says.
"Your tears did it!
I can see your beautiful
face again!"

Soon the prince
marries Rapunzel.
They are very happy.